Bantam Books in the Choose Your Own Adventure® Series
Ask your bookseller for the books you have missed

OUTLAWS OF SHERWOOD FOREST

BY ELLEN KUSHNER

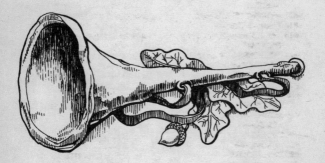

ILLUSTRATED BY JUDITH MITCHELL

A Packard/Montgomery Book

BANTAM BOOKS
TORONTO • NEW YORK • LONDON • SYDNEY • AUCKLAND

For Will Scarlet of Denbigh
and her band of outlaws

RL 5, IL age 10 and up

OUTLAWS OF SHERWOOD FOREST
A Bantam Book / August 1985
2nd printing . . . August 1986

CHOOSE YOUR OWN ADVENTURE® *is a registered trademark of
Bantam Books, Inc. Registered in U.S. Patent and Trademark
Office and elsewhere.*

Original conception of Edward Packard.

Produced by Cloverdale Press Inc.

ISBN 0-553-26388-9

Published simultaneously in the United States and Canada

---

*Bantam Books are published by Bantam Books, Inc. Its trade-
mark, consisting of the words "Bantam Books" and the por-
trayal of a rooster, is Registered in U.S. Patent and Trademark
Office and in other countries. Marca Registrada. Bantam
Books, Inc., 666 Fifth Avenue, New York, New York 10103.*

PRINTED IN THE UNITED STATES OF AMERICA

O   11   10   9   8   7   6   5   4   3

Many speak of Robin Hood
That never bent the bow,
Many talk of Little John
That never did him know.

—Traditional folk song

WARNING!!!!

Do not read this book straight through from beginning to end. These pages contain many different adventures you may have when you're mysteriously transported from summer camp to the Sherwood Forest of Robin Hood's day.

As you read along, you will be able to make choices, and the adventures you have will be the results of those choices: Will you rescue Maid Marian from the evil sheriff of Nottingham? Will you help Robin Hood restore good King Richard to the throne? Will you be able to return to your own time—or will you turn outlaw and live in Sherwood Forest forever?

Think carefully before you make a choice. Then follow the instructions to see what happens to you next. But beware! There are unseen dangers lurking in the shadows of Sherwood Forest.

Camp stinks. Your parents said, "Go, dear. You'll have a wonderful time meeting other kids and roasting marshmallows!" They didn't say anything about giant mosquitoes and cramped cabins and forced swims in ice-cold water. So, like a fool, you went.

The place is called Camp Yoochee-Koowee, but to you it is Camp Yucky-Phooey. Most of the other kids are creeps. Just because this is your first year, they treat you like a second-class citizen, and they're always trying to get you in trouble with the counselors. To make things worse, the food really stinks. Everything is covered with a gooey cream sauce so you can't tell how badly it's been burnt..

You wish you could disapper. Actually. you wish everyone else in the place would disappear, because the area is really kind of pretty. The camp is surrounded by a deep, dark forest, and there's a clear stream running through it. You'd like to walk off into those woods and never come back. But they'd probably call out the dogs or the FBI and corner you like a rat, and the kids would laugh at you, and your parents would cut off your allowance for life. . . .

Turn to page 2.

Only two things make life bearable: your new camera and archery practice. The camera was a birthday present from your parents. It's a Pocket Instamatic with a built-in flash, and you carry it with you everywhere. Archery is great because you turn out to be very, very good at it—the best in camp. And Judy, the archery coach, says that if you keep practicing hard, you'll soon be as good as she is.

Today you've got permission to skip team sports so you can practice some more. You have five white arrows in your quiver, and your sixth is notched and ready. You aim carefully. Just as you release the shot, a soccer ball comes flying from the nearby field and hits you in the back.

Turn to page 4.

As you concentrate on the number three, Raven and the scene around you fade. You remember that three is supposed to be a magic number. But just thinking about it shouldn't do all this! It must be more of the Fair Folk's mischief.

Another scene is coming into focus, like one of those Polaroid pictures that develop in front of your eyes. You see trees and hear someone calling you. . . . You're back in the woods near the archery field!

Confusedly, you remember something about a riddle. Then the memory fades completely. What's really important is your lost arrow. You *could* come back and look for it at night, when the arts and crafts counselor isn't calling you. But if you hunt for it now, by sunlight, it might be easier to find.

Turn to page 17.

4

Your shot goes wild, and your favorite arrow flies off into the woods. There's nothing to do but go search for it.

Fifteen minutes later you're still looking. In the distance you can hear the arts and crafts counselor yelling that it's time to go make igloos out of popsicle sticks. If you ignore her and keep looking, you may get into trouble. But if you leave the arrow in the woods overnight, the morning dew will ruin it. Maybe you could wait till everyone's asleep, then sneak back and search for the arrow by moonlight.

If you keep looking for your arrow,
turn to page 17.

If you decide to hunt for it by moonlight,
turn to page 6.

You start to run, but a fierce pain burns your leg. You fall to the ground and see an arrow buried in the grass beside you. A man comes running up to you. He's dressed all in green, and he's carrying an enormous bow. His arrow has cut the side of your leg.

"Stop!" he cries. "If you run it will be the worse for you."

"You're telling me!" you say. But maybe you can reason with this lunatic. "Listen, I'm bleeding. Have you got a first-aid kit?"

"I know not of this *firstade*," he says. "Why do you trespass in my forest?"

"Look," you explain, "I'm not a trespasser. I'm from camp Yucky-Phooey—I mean Camp Yoo-chee-Koowee."

But even as you speak everything goes dark again. When you can see, you're lying in the clearing, in the middle of the circle of flowers. The man and his arrow have disappeared!

Turn to page 107.

6

When everyone's asleep, you sneak out of your cabin. The full moon makes everything shine silver blue. But the forest looks dark and scary. You're not sure you want to enter it—arrow or no arrow. To give yourself courage, you get your bow and some arrows from the sports shed. Then you begin your search.

. Before long you come to a clearing circled with flowers. A birch tree gleams in the moonlight on the far side. And it suddenly occurs to you that you'll never know if you're *really* good at archery unless you shoot at something besides straw-backed targets—something more difficult, like that birch.

You fit an arrow to your bow and take careful aim. Just as you shoot, a cloud passes in front of the moon. Everything goes dark, but you hear a *thunk*. And when you can see again, you see your arrow quivering in the tree. Fantastic! You're about to see if you can do it again, when you hear a hissing sound. Another arrow has split yours down the middle!

You whirl around. No one's there. You seem to be alone in the moonlit clearing. But *someone* must have shot that arrow. And whoever he is, he's a better marksman than you, and his next arrow may be pointed straight at your heart.

---

*If you take your chance and run for cover,
turn to page 5.*

*If you put down your bow and arrows to show
you mean no harm, turn to page 10.*

Using your bow to push aside the tree branches, you try to make your way back to camp. But nothing looks familiar, and now you're really tired. Finally you reach a clearing: rich green grass dotted with flowers, the perfect place to rest. Gratefully you sink to the ground. That's funny, you think. The flowers seem to be growing in a circle! But they smell wonderful. Bees are humming, the sun is warm . . . before you know it, you're asleep.

Go on to the next page.

You open your eyes to find you're not alone. A tall, bearded man is standing on the other side of the clearing. He's dressed all in green, with high leather boots, and he doesn't look like the sort of person your counselors would want you to associate with.

You're about to run when he calls out, "Hold, knave! Are you a fool to trespass here in Sherwood Forest, or do you flee from the sheriff of Nottingham?"

Sherwood Forest? Nottingham? This guy must be nuts! Oh, you know the legend of Robin Hood and his band of outlaws. They lived in Sherwood Forest, and they were always being chased by the cruel sheriff of the nearby town of Nottingham. But that was supposed to be hundreds of years ago, in medieval England. And it was only a story . . . wasn't it?

You're not sure what's going on, but you'd better give the big man an answer. He's holding a bow about twice the size of yours.

If you think it's best to play along with him, turn to page 14.

If you think your only hope is to run, turn to page 63.

You put down your weapons and stand there, defenseless, in the moonlight. It's the hardest thing you've ever done. Nothing happens. The forest is silent. But you're sure you're not alone. The weird emptiness makes you think of the astronauts on the moon.

"I come in peace for all mankind," you say. Your throat is so dry it comes out a croak. But there's a rustling in the trees, and a form detaches itself from the dappled shadows. It is a man carrying a bow as tall as he is.

"Now, by my faith, that was well said!" he remarks. " 'Peace for all mankind'—a noble thought. But not very likely when our good King Richard is off fighting the Crusades and fair England is bled dry by fat bishops and wicked princes! Come, friend, I see your tongue is as skilled as your hand—what business have you with Robin Hood?"

Turn to page 16.

You join the men who will help Little John "relieve" the tax collector of the people's gold. Because things may get rough, and you've never been in a battle before, John posts you up in a tree at the edge of the forest. When you see the tax collector entering Sherwood, you're supposed to blow a birdcall whistle to warn the outlaws, who are hidden deeper in the forest among the thick trees.

Soon you see a trail of dust on the Nottingham road. It turns out to be a troop of armed guards. A man in fine clothes rides in their midst, his saddlebags bulging. It's the tax collector, and he's well guarded.

He stops his horse right under your tree. You hold your breath, thinking hard. Obviously, you can't give the signal while he's right there. Maybe you could do something even better: jump down on top of him, push him off the horse, and ride away with all the gold yourself! It's a trick you saw on TV—it didn't look hard, and it worked just great. On the other hand, you're new to this outlaw business. Maybe you'd better stick to the original plan and blow the whistle once the tax collector enters the forest.

If you try to capture the gold single-handedly, turn to page 28.

If you choose to stick to Little John's plan, turn to page 74.

"Please, sir," you say, "I'd like to join your band and live in Sherwood Forest."

Robin smiles. "Good! Then pick up your bow and place your right hand upon it. Now, do you swear to steal only from the rich, to give to the poor, and to never betray a fellow outlaw, by the strength of your right hand and your hope of Heaven?"

You feel a chill run up your back at the solemn words. "I do," you say proudly.

"It is well!" He claps you on the shoulder in a comradely fashion. "Then follow me to our secret camp, where you can meet the others."

Robin Hood moves swiftly through the forest. His feet never make a sound, although every step you take makes a noise like an elephant crunching a ton of peanut shells!

At the outlaw camp, you are made welcome. Little John is there, along with many of the band. You meet Friar Tuck, Alan-a-Dale, and a cheerful red-haired man called Will Scarlett. There is a big fire, with a whole deer roasting over it. Someone cuts you a slice. It's delicious. You have to eat it with your fingers, but no one seems to mind when the juice runs down your chin.

Across the fire from you is an old man. His hair and beard are long and white, and his features are in shadow. But his eyes glimmer like stars.

"Who's that?" you ask Will Scarlett, pointing to the old man.

"Where? That's Little John."

"No, in front of him."

Will gives you a funny look. "There's no one

there," he says. "Now, come; Robin's making
plans for tomorrow's raids. You don't want to be
left out, do you?" He hurries off.

You look back across the fire. The old man is
still there, smiling strangely at you.

If you go after Will, turn to page 22.

*If you decide to investigate the mysterious old
man first, turn to page 99.*

14

You think fast. The man is awfully tall. If this is supposed to be Sherwood Forest, and he's one of Robin Hood's men, then he must be . . .

"Little John!" you say. "I'm so glad to find you."

"Oh, are you?" he says. "And what business have you with John Little, that some do call Little John?"

You've guessed right! And he's answered, just as in the books. As you recall, at this point you're supposed to make a stirring speech about having traveled far to join the merry band and live in liberty under the greenwood, righting wrong and fighting injustice. So you do.

Little John looks happy. "Well spoken," he says. "You are welcome here in Sherwood. Poor little child! These be sad times, sad times indeed. You all alone and not even knowing better than to sleep in a fairy ring!" He indicates the circle of flowers. "They say if you fall asleep inside one of these rings, the Fair Folk may carry you off to some strange enchanted land!"

Turn to page 21.

You're determined to get Raven's voice back, but before you ask the queen for any favors, you'd better butter her up. You bow low and say, "Gracious lady, forgive my rude disbelief. The tales told in my time don't do justice to your beauty and majesty."

The corner of the queen's mouth quirks in a pleased smile.

"Your Majesty," you continue, "I beg you to grant me this request: Give my friend Raven back his gift of song!"

"Is that all, bold mortal?" she asks. "You wish nothing for yourself?"

"Well, yes," you confess. "But Raven first."

She looks closely at you. "You are unusually generous for one of your kind. Most mortals are quick to ask favors only for themselves. You please me well, and I will grant you the wish of your heart."

"But what about Raven?" you ask.

"Ah," says the queen, "but you see, he did *not* please me."

There is a moment of darkness, then you suddenly find yourself sitting on your bed at camp. Your counselor is telling you to hurry up, because the bus leaves for home in an hour. No one seems to have noticed that you've been gone the last three weeks. The queen of the Fair Folk has truly granted you the wish of your heart: Camp is over!

The End

16

Robin Hood! You can't believe it. "But Robin Hood was an English outlaw in the middle ages," you say. "He died hundreds of years ago!"

The tall man laughs as though you'd made a really good joke. "Did I indeed, young friend? I wish you would tell that to the sheriff of Nottingham; maybe then he and his knights would stop chasing me and leave sweet Sherwood Forest in peace."

"The wicked sheriff!" you say, remembering the stories.

"Indeed he is a wicked man," says Robin Hood. "I see you are no friend to him, and thus are friend to me. Now, will you join my band of outlaws, or may I escort you to the other side of Sherwood Forest?"

The man seems real enough. Somehow, someway, you've been transported to the past.

If you decide to join Robin Hood's band, turn to page 12.

If you'd like to try your fortune in some other part of merry old England, turn to page 43.

Ignoring the arts and crafts counselor's insistent calling, you plunge deeper into the woods, your eyes on the undergrowth. Still no arrow. Could you really have shot it this far?

The trees are close together in this part of the forest, and it's hard to push your way between them. You're getting hot and sticky. Maybe it's time to give up and go back.

But when you turn around, you can't even see the archery field. Vainly you try to remember whether moss grows on the north or south side of trees. Not that it would help. You don't know which direction Camp Yoochee-Koowee is anyway. What you are is lost.

Turn to page 7.

You walk quickly back to the tables, leaving the other page behind. There are dogs everywhere, waiting for people to throw them bones. You try to be careful, but a sudden yelp lets you know you've stepped on one's tail. A lady in gold turns around and hits you on the side of your head with a huge loaf of bread.

"Clumsy oaf! Take care!" She picks up the dog, cooing, "Did mummy's precious darling get hurt?"

Your ear is still ringing with the blow when the lady shrieks, "Don't just stand there, you fool! Go fetch my cloak—and be quick about it!"

Clearly a *real* page would know where she kept her cloak. But for you, it's the perfect excuse to leave the hall without being questioned. While that awful woman waits all night for her cloak, you can take the opportunity to learn your way around the castle.

You go down a long corridor that ends in a door. Next to it is a staircase leading upward.

If you open the door, turn to page 41.

If you go up the stairs, turn to page 108.

You feel a jerk on the rope. Sir Guy has reached the window, and he has begun to haul you up. You take a deep breath and let go.

You hit the moat with a big splash. The water is murky and green. Marian's skirts are dragging you down. You struggle to get out of the gown, but it's hopeless.

If only you hadn't fallen asleep in the fairy ring, none of this would have happened. Okay, Fair Folk, you think. If you ever wanted to help me, now's the time!

Nothing happens. The water swirls around your eyes as you sink. . . .

Turn to page 103.

You can't believe a grown man is warning you about little fairies, and you tell him so.

Little John looks serious. "Hereabouts we know better than to offend the Fair Folk—the Good People. They don't much like the word"—he whispers very softly—"*fairies.* Now let's be gone from this magic place before they hear us using That Word and decide to do us some mischief."

He really means it! And you have to admit that, so far, it's the only explanation for your presence here. You think for a moment. If this really *is* Sherwood Forest, and people believe in magic, you could become famous. After all, you come from the twentieth century, where there's advanced technology! You could set yourself up as the king's advisor, or even as a great wizard!

Lost in daydreams you follow Little John through the forest. "I fear you've come at a sad time," he tells you. "There's terrible trouble."

"What is it?" you ask.

But he only sighs and says, "Nothing a mere child like you could help with."

If there's one thing you can't stand, it's being told you're just a kid who can't do anything useful.

If you tell Little John you're really a powerful wizard in disguise, turn to page 59.

If you decide to show him that a mere child can still be a good archer, turn to page 34.

After a moment's hesitation, you hurry after Will Scarlett and the other outlaws.

"Oh," says Will. "There you are. We thought you'd been carried off by old Nilrem."

"Who's that?" you ask.

"He's a mysterious character who's supposed to haunt Sherwood, giving people strange advice. Some say he's a wizard, some say he's one of the Fair Folk. *I* say he's a product of one too many mugs of ale."

You start to say something about the old man. But Robin Hood is beginning to speak, and you turn to listen.

"My merry men: I have word that the royal tax collector will be passing through Sherwood tomorrow noon—laden with bags of gold. He will be guarded by an escort of soldiers, but with our knowledge of the wood we can set a trap for them. I cannot promise there will be no danger, but Little John is in command of the raid, and he needs volunteers. I, myself, will go to Brampton as usual, to bring the poor there the gold I have promised them."

"Oh, no you won't," says a voice.

The band of outlaws gasps, and Robin shakes his fist. "Who dares to contradict Robin Hood?" he demands.

Turn to page 35.

You got yourself into this mess, and you're determined to get yourself out of it. You throw your whistle deep into the underbrush, so your captors can't use it to give your outlaw friends a false signal.

The captain of the guards ties you up and slings you across his saddle facedown. Horse hair gets in your nose, and something in the saddle is jabbing into your stomach.

"I'll take the little thief back to Nottingham for trial," says the captain.

"No," the tax collector says. "I need all my guards to get through the forest safely. Thieves are always hanged, anyway; let's do it now and save time."

You gulp. Then, all of a sudden, you realize what's jabbing you in the stomach. It's not the saddle at all, it's your pocket camera! And this piece of twentieth-century magic may be just the thing to save you!

"Stop!" you cry. "Lay one filthy finger on me, and you won't live long enough to regret it. I am the keeper of powerful magic. I am a dangerous witch!"

"That's different," says the tax collector. "Witches are burned alive. We haven't time for that. I guess we'll have to send you back to Nottingham for trial after all."

Turn to page 31.

You do a double somersault and come up smiling. The fat man laughs some more. "Oho!" he says. "You make me forget all my troubles with the outlaw Robin Hood! In fact, you almost make me forget I'm sheriff of Nottingham!"

So *this* is the evil sheriff! You tell him, "I am the greatest clown in the world! If you let me stay here, I will entertain you." And, you're thinking, I will figure out a way to rescue Maid Marian.

The sheriff likes your clowning so much he keeps you with him all the time. You don't think much of someone whose favorite sight is a little old lady falling flat on her face, but he treats you well. The problem is, you never have a chance to get near Marian's tower.

One day while you're clowning for the sheriff— ducking the fruit he throws at you—you hear the guards crying, "Help! Attack!" It seems Robin Hood has grown tired of waiting.

A troop of archers runs into the room, led by Little John. When he sees you alive and well and with the sheriff, he cries, "False friend! Traitor!"

You try to tell him, "I was doing my best." But the words fade in your throat as he sends an arrow through you.

The End

Smoke is pouring steadily into the church and you're beginning to cough, but you'll stay with Robin.

"Down on the floor!" he orders. "The smoke will rise to the ceiling, and the air will be sweeter below."

You both lie flat. The floor is stone and very cold, and you feel a lump under your shoulder. It's an iron ring, set in the floor—though you can't imagine why.

"We will wait until they open the doors to fetch us out," Robin says. "They will think me weak with smoke, but there is always strength in my right arm to fight for freedom! We may yet see a happy end to this bad day."

"Yeah," you say. You've only been half listening, because you're aware of footsteps. It sounds as though someone were walking up a stone staircase—right under your head!

Turn to page 47.

"Shame on you!" you cry. "Who taught you to laugh at poor old ladies?"

"But"—he sputters —"but I'm the sheriff of Nottingham!"

The wicked sheriff himself! It's too late to back out now. You remember what Little John said about the nurse. "I don't care if you're the sheriff of Timbuktu—you should have better manners, young man! I don't know what kind of home you were brought up in, but in *my* day we had a little respect for poor helpless old women."

"I'm sorry," the sheriff says, looking sheepish. He helps you up, dusts you off, and then—to your delight—slinks off down the hall, looking ashamed of himself.

The guard unlocks the door to Marian's room. Inside, a lady in green is doing chin-ups on the top beam of a big tapestry loom.

"I'll be back in ten minutes to let you out," says the guard. He locks the door behind him, leaving you alone with the athletic lady—who is regarding you with a very suspicious eye.

Turn to page 76.

Holding your breath, you drop from the tree and land on the tax collector's back. "Give me the gold," you growl, "or I'll—" Of course you don't have a knife, but you jab your whistle into the man's side and hope it's convincing.

He screams. "Take the gold! Take it! Spare my life!"

Aha, you think. This isn't so hard after all.

"Or you'll what?" says the captain of the guard, picking you up by the scruff of your shirt. "Play 'Greensleeves' off-key?"

He has called your bluff, and now you have to think fast. If you blow your whistle extra loud, Little John may realize something's wrong and come to your rescue. But if you do, you'll alert the tax collector to the trap and blow the outlaws' chance of a surprise attack.

If you risk facing your captors alone,
turn to page 23.

If you signal for help, turn to page 80.

The man in green lets you down out of the tree.
Then he shoots an arrow straight across the clearing. "There's your target," he says. "Hit it—or
come as close as you can."

Hit it? You can barely *see* it! But you aim carefully . . . and shoot.

To your amazement, not only does your arrow
land right next to his, but it nicks his arrow's
feathers!

"Truly a marvelous display!" says the man.

"Beginner's luck," you mutter under your
breath.

"You have ruined an arrow in Robin Hood's
quiver," the man says. "Yet I count it no loss, for
you shall be my new arrow!" He slaps you on
the back.

You can't believe it. You have shot against Robin Hood himself!

"Follow me," says Robin. "We'll join the rest
of my merry band deep in Sherwood Forest."

Turn to page 12.

Maybe old Nilrem *could* have helped you, but there's nothing you can do about it now. Just in case, though, you yell, "Nilrem! Save me!"

The guards mutter uncomfortably, "A witch, indeed, that calls upon wizards and Fair Folk for aid. Come, let us light the fire—and quickly!"

They do.

The End

The captain of the guard carries you back to Nottingham. He is so afraid of your magical powers that he never even unties your hands. You wonder if Little John and the outlaws were able to surprise the tax collector. But at the moment, you're more concerned about the nasty surprises that might await you!

In Nottingham you are thrown into a dungeon. Things do not look good. It seems as if you'll either be hanged as a thief or burned as a witch.

Go on to the next page.

You waste away in jail for weeks. Finally the sheriff sends for you. He is a fat man with little narrow eyes. His purple velvet clothes are spattered with grease stains.

"So you claim you are a witch," he says. "Can you prove it?"

"Why should I?" you ask. "You'll only burn me."

"Not necessarily." He smiles an oily smile. "I could use a witch. Not even the king has one. But it all depends on how powerful you really are."

Is he telling you the truth?

If you try to impress him with your powers, turn to page 114.

If you tell him you're not really a witch, turn to page 95.

"Please don't argue, Marian," you say sternly. "This may be your only chance. Anyhow, I'm not really this fat." You pull the stuffing out of your disguise. "Part of this is a rope. I'm going to escape once you're safely away." Before she can insist that *she* use the rope while *you* get out the safe way, you take off the old-lady clothes.

Marian disguises herself as the nurse, and you struggle into her long gown. Just as you're doing the last button, the guard comes to the door. You turn your back and look out the window so he can't see your face. And Marian hides hers in a handkerchief. It works! Marian leaves with him. You hear the "old nurse" crying and sobbing about "Marian" all the way down the hall.

With Marian on her way, you turn your attention to your escape plan. You are in the highest tower, about five stories above the ground. There's a deep moat below, and you're not sure your rope is really long enough.

There's a knock on the door. "Who is it?" you ask, trying to sound like Marian.

" 'Tis Guy of Gisborne, your own true love," a voice answers.

You want to give Marian a chance to get safely away from the castle. But now might be the time to use the ladder. If Guy finds out you're a fake, you could be in real trouble!

If you decide to escape now, turn to page 39.

If you decide to stall for time, turn to page 94.

"I may be young, but maybe I *can* help," you say to Little John. "At least let me try! Look, I can shoot—" You fit arrow to bowstring and hit a distant birch tree.

"Well shot!" he cries. "By Saint Sebastian, perhaps we can use you after all." Then he looks worried. "Still, you are but a child. If any harm should come to you . . ."

You grit your teeth. "Never mind about that. Tell me what's happened."

Little John finds paths through a forest that looks like pure wilderness to you. As you walk he tells you that Maid Marian, Robin Hood's own true love, has been captured by the sheriff of Nottingham. The evil sheriff was Marian's guardian until she fell in love with Robin and ran off to the greenwood. Now that the sheriff has her back in his clutches, he is going to force her to marry Sir Guy of Gisborne. He vows that she'll never see Robin again. And to make sure she can't get away this time, he has locked her in the highest tower of his castle. So it looks as if Robin and his band will have to launch a full-scale attack to rescue her.

If you volunteer to join the attack on the castle, turn to page 68.

If you think a secret rescue operation would work better, turn to page 62.

"I dare," says Friar Tuck, pushing forward. "I hear there have been spies in Brampton— strangers asking about Robin Hood. It might be the sheriff's men have set a trap for you. And I say, send someone else or, if you must go, at least take one of our band with you to be lookout. Let it be one of the new recruits, someone who won't be recognized as one of us."

"You strike a hard bargain, but so be it, Tuck." Robin flings up his arm heroically. "Now, who's for Little John and the tax collector's gold, and who's for me and the poor of Brampton, and who"—he laughs—"wants to stay by the fire all day and get fat?"

All around you men are stepping forward, offering to go with Little John. You're about to join them when Will Scarlett nudges you.

"Here's your chance," he says. "Your face is not yet known in Brampton. You could go with Robin Hood."

*If you offer to go with Little John,
turn to page 11.*

*If you volunteer to go with Robin Hood,
turn to page 72.*

Little John finds you the clothing of a castle page. You put it on and follow him to the gate of Nottingham Castle.

"Remember," he whispers before he leaves, "you've got to get Marian out soon, or she'll be married to Sir Guy! If we don't see you in Sherwood by Whitsunday, we'll have to attack the castle—even if you're still inside! Now, go on, and may the luck of the Fair Folk be with you!"

It's lunchtime in the castle, and people are scurrying around the big dining hall like mad. Sure enough, no one notices an extra page. They make you carry food to the sheriff and his friends at the high table, pour out wine, and take away dirty dishes. Being a page is like being a waiter, except that you don't get any tips. You don't get to eat, either! All this running around is making you very hungry, and you're thirsty, too. Finally someone hands you a bowl of sweet-smelling water to put on the table. It isn't exactly Kool-Aid, but it's better than wine. Slipping behind a pillar, you take a nice long drink.

Suddenly a voice behind you cries, "What are you *doing?* That's rose water—it's for washing your hands!"

Go on to the next page.

It's another page, a boy with freckles and a gap between his front teeth. "You'd better come with me," he says.

Can you trust him? If he finds out you're an impostor he might turn you in. But you could sure use help, and it would be nice to have a friend.

*If you try to get away from him,
turn to page 19.*

If you go with him, turn to page 54.

After almost a week, you take Clarence aside. He could be a big help in your rescue mission, but you don't dare tell him the truth right away. Instead you make up a story to see where his sympathies lie.

"Clarence, remember you asked me what I was in trouble for the night we first met? Well, I'll tell you: I was trying to sneak up to the tower to see Maid Marian. I only did it for the adventure, but they caught me and made me go without supper."

Clarence looks grave. "You're lucky they didn't lock you up!" he says. "No one may visit the lady until she's married to Sir Guy of Gisborne."

"I know," you say. "But aren't you even the least bit curious about her? Don't you want to know what she looks like?"

Clarence shakes his head. "I want to be a knight more than anything else in the world," he says. "Why should I risk that to see a lady who got herself captured?"

Clarence has a point. The life of a knight is very appealing, and you'd forfeit your chance to be one—maybe even your life—if you were caught trying to rescue Marian. On the other hand, this mission was your idea, and you'd hate to let Little John and Robin down. There must be something you can say to convince Clarence to help you.

If you decide to give up your mission and continue training as a knight, turn to page 66.

If you try to get Clarence to help you rescue Marian, turn to page 71.

With shaking hands you tie one end of the rope to a ring in the wall. "Just a minute," you call to Sir Guy, "I'm—um—fixing my hair!"

"I can wait," he says in a smooth voice, "for soon you will be mine, all mine. And once we are joined forever in the bonds of holy—"

The rest of his speech is lost as you begin to lower yourself out the window. You don't dare look down. Your sweating hands are slippery on the rope. The skirts of Marian's gown are getting in your way. If only you can escape undetected!

Suddenly you hear a voice from the roof shouting, "Marian's escaping! Stop her!"

Turn to page 20.

When you wake up, it is night and the full moon is shining brightly. You must have fallen asleep instead of looking for your arrow. And what a strange dream you had—all about Robin Hood.

You decide you'd better get back to camp, put your bow back in the sports shack, and sneak back into your cabin. Then you notice that it's not your camp bow that's in your hand—it's an old, old hunting horn!

Somehow, you don't think there's much point in showing it to the camp directors or explaining how you left valuable camp property in Sherwood Forest. Besides, you're planning to go back and get the bow and arrows just as soon as you can figure out how.

The End

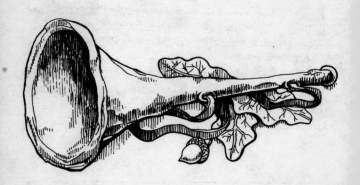

The door leads out into a large courtyard. Across from you is a great big gate, and someone is pounding on it from the outside. "Who goes there?" calls the sheriff's guard.

"Open in the name of Prince John!" a voice replies. "His Majesty dines with the sheriff of Nottingham tonight."

You watch from the shadows as the guards work the enormous pulley system that opens the gate. All the while you're trying to remember what you've heard about Prince John. In the Robin Hood story he was the bad guy. His older brother, Richard the Lionheart, went off to fight in the Crusades and left him to rule England. At dinner you overheard someone mutter, "When King Richard returns, Prince John will have a lot to explain!" And you recall that John oppressed the poor—with the sheriff of Nottingham's help. Well, if Robin was against John and for Richard, you'd better be, too.

Prince John seems to be leading an entire procession into Nottingham Castle. Behind him come knights, squires, nobles, minstrels, jugglers, and guards. Bringing up the parade is a group of barefoot friars.

You realize you've still got your Pocket Instamatic with you. What a picture this would make! But what if someone sees you take it?

If you decide to take a picture, turn to page 91.

If you decide it's too risky, turn to page 56.

You stare boldly at the queen of the Fair Folk.
"Your Majesty," you say, "I can't do magic tricks
like you. But all your riddle needs is a little
logic to solve it. Here's my answer: When I hunted
for my arrow under the rays of the moon, I came
here. So if I'd hunted under the rays of the sun,
I'd be somewhere else now!"

The lady's eyes narrow. "Very clever. Very
clever indeed. You have played the riddle game
with me, mortal, and you have won. The rules
bind me to my word, and I must keep it. I will
send you back to the twentieth century."

Before you can even say good-bye to Raven,
the world begins to spin . . . you close your eyes
in dizziness. You hear the jingle of silver bells,
louder and louder, until suddenly all is silent.

You open your eyes—and there you are,
standing on your own front doorstep. Camp is
over and you're home!

You ring the doorbell. After a while the lock
clicks, and a white-haired man opens the door.
He stares at you as though he doesn't believe his
eyes.

It takes you a moment to recognize your own
father. Then you see the date on the newspaper
in his hand: August 1, 1999!

The queen has kept her word and sent you
back to your own century. But this isn't quite what
you had in mind. . . .

The End

"Thanks," you tell Robin Hood, "I guess I *would* like to see what else is happening around here."

Swiftly and silently, Robin Hood leads you through the forest. Dawn is breaking as you come to the edge of the woods. You see a road, well-tended fields, and cattle grazing. A man is walking down the road, and he has a small harp slung across his back.

"Well," says Robin, "it seems your first adventure will be musical."

You turn to say good-bye, but he has already vanished into the forest. You step out onto the road, right in front of the minstrel.

Go on to the next page.

"Oh, dear," the minstrel says softly. "Are the outlaws grown so bold that they leave Sherwood to attack innocent travelers on the road?"

You realize you are still carrying your bow and arrows. "I'm not a thief," you reassure him. "And I mean you no harm."

"Good," he replies. "After all, I have only this harp. And while I'm sure you pluck a bowstring very nicely, harp strings require a little more skill."

"I don't want your harp," you say. "I'm on the road looking for adventure. Let me come with you. I can protect you from robbers."

"Indeed?" he says with a smile. "Well, I'm only adventuring the long way around the forest, to Nottingham Castle. There's to be a wedding there in a week or two, and minstrels are popular at weddings. I'll gladly accept your protection, if you'll accept a position as my apprentice in return. I'll teach you to play the harp, and if you've any kind of voice, I'll be more than glad to let you sing for people when I play. But if you'd rather apprentice yourself to a knight, I passed one not a mile down the road."

*If you agree to go with the minstrel,
turn to page 75.*

*If you decide to go look for the knight,
turn to page 82.*

While pretending to put money in Robin's beggar's bowl, you lean over and whisper, "I saw someone watching you from the corner of the church. Then he slipped away. I think he might be up to something."

Before Robin can answer, you hear a horn and the thunder of hooves. Five men on horseback sweep into the town, their swords drawn and raised.

"In the name of the sheriff of Nottingham and of Prince John of England, we come to arrest the outlaw Robin Hood," one shouts. "Let no man hinder us, on peril of his life!"

Robin carries a sword under his rags, but he can't fight off five men without help. Across the square is the blacksmith's shop, full of half-finished swords, horseshoes, and iron bars. You're sure to find a weapon there. But can you reach the shop in time?

"Quick!" Robin whispers. "Into the church and lock the door!"

*If you follow Robin into the church,
turn to page 55.*

*If you run to the blacksmith's shop to get a
weapon, turn to page 98.*

The footsteps get louder. Quickly you stand up. "Down!" hisses Robin, but the stone you were lying on begins to move. Someone is lifting it from below. You grab the iron ring and give a heave.

The head of a very old man appears. His hair is all wispy and his eyes are a pale watery blue. "Thank you," he says politely. "It is so hard for me to lift the stone these days. But I must come to the church to visit my brothers and pray. I am Brother Sebastian. May I ask what you're doing here?"

"We are trying to escape arrest, good friar," Robin says.

"Oh, are you criminals?" he asks. "I am very much afraid of criminals."

"Not criminals, good friar, but outlaws fleeing injustice," Robin replies.

"Ah," the old man says slowly. "That's different, isn't it? I can help you escape through my secret tunnel. But it's very narrow. I can only take you through one at a time." He stares at you with his strange, watery eyes.

Brother Sebastian seems very odd, and who knows what dangers his tunnel may hold! But going with him might be better than taking your chances with the soldiers.

If you decide to risk Brother Sebastian's tunnel, turn to page 84.

If you decide to stay in the church, turn to page 113.

Marian has come up with a plan that will let both of you escape. "The sheriff just left me to get some ink," she says. "He wants me to sign a paper saying I agree to marry Sir Guy. You stand behind the door, and when he comes back, hit him over the head with this bass recorder. Then I'll change into his clothes, make myself look fat by stuffing them with tapestry yarn, and we'll escape together in disguise!"

"But you don't look a bit like the sheriff," you object.

"Don't worry, I'll cover my face," she says. "Now—hide yourself. I hear him coming!"

Go on to the next page.

One good knock on the head, and the sheriff goes out like a light. Marian changes into his fancy clothes and wraps a cloth around her face, as if it were a bandage for a sore tooth. As the two of you go out the door, she leans her head on your shoulder, moaning.

"His Excellency has a bit of a toothache," you tell the guards. "But don't worry, old nurse is going to fix him up. Come along, young man. If you didn't eat so many sweets you wouldn't be in this fix, and you wouldn't be so fat, either."

Once you're outside the castle and into the forest, you and Marian laugh so hard you can barely breathe! Then she leads you to the outlaw camp.

Robin Hood is delighted that you've rescued Marian. He declares a feast in your honor and insists you take a bag of gold as a reward. The outlaws beg you to stay and join their band. Robin says he'll give you archery lessons, and Marian promises to teach you how to move silently in the woods. In the end you decide to stay. You have become an outlaw of Sherwood Forest.

The End

Robin Hood gives you his horn to summon help once you reach the forest. Then, very carefully, you squeeze yourself through the window and drop silently to the ground. No one sees you. The sheriff's men are all at the front of the church, waiting for Robin Hood to come out. You creep around the edge of the town, then run toward the cover of the woods.

You run so hard there's a terrible stitch in your side by the time you reach Sherwood. With your last breath you blow Robin's hunting horn. In a moment the outlaws come running. When you tell them what's happened, they set off at once for Brampton to rescue their leader.

Still panting from your desperate run, you lie down on the forest floor in the middle of a circle of sweet-smelling flowers. You only mean to rest for a moment, but soon you are asleep.

Turn to page 40.

You rack your brains for a good excuse. But luckily no one seems to expect you to challenge the Black Knight. After all, it's unlikely that you would beat him at the game when grown men have failed. For once you're not sorry to be considered a "mere child."

"By Our Lady," says Robin Hood, "I know of only one man who could defeat so many. But, alas, he is far across the sea."

"Who do you mean?" the knight asks.

"I mean our good King Richard, who is away fighting in the Crusades," says Robin. "He is sorely missed at home, for his brother Prince John is a tyrant."

"Beware," the knight says. "What you speak is treason."

Robin laughs. "Not while I rule in Sherwood! Here any friend of Richard's is a friend to me, and his enemies are my enemies!"

"Then bid me welcome, friend," says the Black Knight, taking off his helmet.

Robin Hood and his outlaws go down on their knees. It is King Richard.

Turn to page 64.

The old man told you there were words of power that would get you home—words of your own making. What are they?

"Abracadabra!" You yell the only magic words you know. Nothing. "Please and thank you! Walt Disney! Kirk to Enterprise! Open Sesame Street!" Still nothing.

"These are words of sorcery," the sheriff cries. "Quick, light the fires!"

Guards are approaching with flaming torches. "Oh," you cry, "I wish I were back in Camp Yoo-chee-Koowee—oh, Yucky-Phooey!"

Suddenly there is a blinding blaze of light, like one hundred Instamatic flashes all going off at once. When you can see again, you are lying on the grass of the archery field. The magic words must have been *Yucky-Phooey.*

A light is coming toward you—but it's only a flashlight. The counselors are all out looking for you. You're going to be in big trouble for sneaking out after dark, but it's better than being burned at the stake! Maybe camp isn't so bad after all.

And maybe that picture you took of the sheriff of Nottingham will come out. . . .

The End

Holding the half-empty bowl of rose water, you follow the page out into the hall. You're afraid he's going to tell on you. But he only takes you to a bucket and refills your bowl with plain water.

"They'll never notice the difference," he says. "My name's Clarence. Did they make you go without supper as a punishment? What did you do? You must have been pretty desperate to drink rose water. I have some bread and cheese. I'll share it with you if you'll tell me what you did wrong. Or did you do it on a dare? Make haste— we must get back to the hall before we're missed!"

You like Clarence. He asks a lot of questions, but luckily he's always too busy talking to wait for the answers. In the days that follow, he becomes your close friend, and always helps you out if you get confused.

The life of a page isn't so bad, once you get the hang of it. You have to wait on the nobles, but in return you will be taught how to be a knight. Clarence's cousin is a knight, and your new friend tells you how exciting it will be to have your own horse and sword and to ride in tournaments. Every morning the pages have weapons practice. You're learning how to handle a sword, and everyone is impressed with your skill in archery.

Your days are very busy, and you're too exhausted to search the castle at night. But you haven't forgotten your mission: to rescue Maid Marian.

Turn to page 38.

You and Robin Hood lock the church door behind you and bar the shutters on the windows.

The sheriff's men pound on the door, yelling threats, but Robin says you're safe. "They will not harm us here in the sanctuary of the church," he explains. "But I must think what to do. We cannot stay here forever. If we are lucky, one of the Brampton folk will run to Sherwood to ask my men for help. But we cannot count on that."

While Robin tries to work out a plan, you prowl around the church. Then you smell smoke.

"The curs!" Robin cries. "They have set green wood alight around the church to smoke us out. In an hour there will be no air left to breathe. Alas, it is a sorry day for England when such fiends represent the king's justice!"

"It will be a sorry day for *us* if we don't get out of here," you say. "I found a tiny window at the back of the church. Maybe they aren't watching it. You can't get through, but *I* can. I'll squeeze through and run to Sherwood for help."

"No," says Robin. "It's too dangerous. They would shoot you on sight—and maybe help is on the way."

If you stay with Robin Hood, turn to page 26.

If you risk going through the window, turn to page 50.

The courtyard is bustling with activity. It would be foolhardy to try and take a picture now.

From your hiding place you watch one of the friars drop out of the procession. Something in the way he moves makes you suspect he hasn't been wearing his robes long. He walks right toward you, and on a hunch you step out of the shadows.

Go on to the next page.

Startled, the friar puts his hand to his side, as though he were carrying a sword. When he sees you're only a page, he draws you back into the shadows and looks you straight in the eyes. He is very handsome. His eyes are piercing, and his face is tanned.

"My child," he says. "Would you serve your king?"

"You mean Prince John?" you say, playing dumb.

"They say King Richard has returned from the Holy Land and stands in need of friends," the friar replies. "What say you to that?"

Suddenly you know who the man must be. It's your big moment, and you play it for all it's worth. "I say, down with wicked Prince John!" you whisper dramatically.

The man smiles. "If you would truly serve the king, see that you serve at the prince's table tonight," he says. "Mark well what passes between him and the sheriff, and if you hear anything suspicious, bring word of it to me."

"How will I find you?" you ask.

He smiles again. "Oh, I'll be at the banquet— enjoying Nottingham's hospitality," he says. "Now, will you do it?"

"Yes, sir—I mean sire," you say. For of course he is King Richard.

Go on to the next page.

You spend the next few hours looking for Marian and learning your way around the castle. No one you ask seems to know anything about her. And you don't want to seem *too* interested, or people will get suspicious.

As the evening draws on, the dining hall fills up for the banquet. You are kept busy fetching and carrying, and the prince's minstrels and jugglers are kept busy performing. There's even a dancing bear!

King Richard is sitting at a low table, still wearing his friar's robes. As you promised, you're keeping an eye on his brother and the sheriff. You're about to set a big bowl of steaming soup on the table when Prince John leans over to the sheriff and says, "They tell me my brother has returned and travels about the country disguised as a friar or a merchant or a Black Knight."

"No merchants here," says the sheriff, busily stuffing his mouth. "Please pass the salt."

"That friar," says Prince John, pointing to Richard. "The one whose hood hides his face. Do you suppose . . ."

You are sure that being recognized is not part of Richard's plan. Somehow you must stop John from speaking to him. You could warn the king of his brother's suspicion. But maybe the soup can provide a distraction.

If you go to warn Richard, turn to page 67.

If you spill the soup in Prince John's lap, turn to page 88.

"Mere child?" you say scornfully. "I'll have you know that I am really a powerful wizard in disguise!"

"Oh, you are, are you?" Little John says. He fits an arrow to his bow and points it at you. "Then back into the Fairy Ring with you, while I decide what to do."

You do as he says. This isn't going the way you hoped. But maybe your Instamatic will impress him. You take the camera out of your pocket. "Beware of rousing a wizard's wrath," you say.

You set the flash and take his picture. For a moment he's shocked. But he's smart enough to realize that all you've done is flash a light without hurting him. You try to follow up with some impressive-sounding magic words: "Alacazam! Zippety zappety zoo!" Nothing happens. You start to feel desperate. *"I before E except after C,"* you babble. *"E equals mc squared!"*

By reciting the law of matter conversion you seem to have triggered something in the fairy ring. Suddenly Little John vanishes, and you are back at camp. The arts and crafts counselor is closing in on you, and you are in big trouble.

Somehow, you make it through the rest of the summer. When you get home, you have your roll of film developed. Among the snapshots is a picture of a tall man in green holding a very large bow.

"Who's that, dear?" your parents ask.

"Oh," you answer, "just a visiting archery expert."

The End

"Okay," you say, swallowing hard. "Now it's my turn to try knocking over the stranger."

"Nay," says the Black Knight. "I do not strike children."

"A noble man," Will Scarlett says sarcastically, rubbing his own bruised arm. "Come, sir, do you fear to be defeated by our small fry? Surely you will give this brave youth a chance to strike at *you*—nobody said you had to hit back!"

"Very well," says the knight. "Come, child, do your best."

You back up to the other end of the clearing and get a running start so you'll have enough strength to push the knight over. As you come barreling across the grass, the outlaws cheer you on as if you're at a track meet. Just before you reach the knight you yell, "Look out! Quick! Behind you!"

Turn to page 70.

"Look," you say to Little John, "there are better ways to solve this than with violence."

"I know." He scratches his head. "There's cunning, stealth, schemes, plots, and disguises."

You like the idea of wearing a disguise; and when John points out that you're just about Marian's size, your plan is born. If you can just get the guards to let you into Marian's room, you can exchange clothes with her. And if you can pretend to be Marian long enough for her to get away, she can escape in your disguise. By the time the sheriff realizes he's got the wrong person, it will be too late. And he can't make you marry Sir Guy!

Little John thinks it's a wonderful idea. Now all you have to do is think of a good disguise. He says, "There's Marian's old nurse. Horrible woman. She could scold the stripes off a tiger. No one would dare to get in her way. Or you could go as one of the castle pages. I know where to get you a uniform, and there are so many pages no one would notice an extra one."

If you think the old nurse is a good disguise, turn to page 104.

If you want to go as a page, turn to page 36.

You scramble to your feet and head for the cover of the woods. As you duck under the first branches, a strong arm swings you up into a tree and pins you there.

"Well, now! Here's a fine deer to catch in Sherwood," says your captor. He is also wearing green and carrying a bow. "Little John," he calls to the other man. "Go back to the camp. I would have a word with this scamp."

These people certainly dress and act like Robin Hood's men! Even if it's only a game it might be fun to play along.

"I have traveled from the dreadful forest of Yoochee-Koowee to join your brave band," you say. "I may seem like a child, but my heart is bold and I am a great archer in my own land." (Well, the archery coach *did* say you were the best in camp.)

If the man laughs, you'll die. Instead he nods thoughtfully and says, "Your words are good, but let us see how well you bend a bow." There is a fierce light in his eyes, and suddenly you wish you'd been a little more modest.

Turn to page 29.

King Richard raises Robin Hood and the other outlaws from their knees. Then he explains that his brother John would like to keep him from taking back the throne and that is why he must go about in disguise. But he feels safer already, knowing that Robin is on his side. He agrees to help rescue Marian from Nottingham Castle.

"But," he says, "let us make no direct attack. Let us disguise ourselves as friars, join the next convoy that seeks to enter the castle, and take the sheriff's men by surprise."

The disguises are arranged. Then you take a position along the road to watch for a large group going toward Nottingham that the "friars" can attach themselves to.

Farmers go by with their carts, and milkmaids pass with their pails. Finally, along comes a large group of people riding horses and talking and laughing.

"Hello," you call to them. "Who are you and where are you going?"

"We are pilgrims on our way to the holy shrine at Canterbury," answers their leader.

"Will you be passing through Nottingham?" you ask.

"Aye," says the leader. "Right under the very walls of the castle."

These pilgrims could give Robin's men cover as far as the city, but they aren't going into the castle itself.

If you give the signal for your "friars" to join the pilgrims, turn to page 115.

If you wait for a group that's going into the castle, turn to page 79.

Now that you are no longer looking for Maid Marian, you are much more comfortable going about your daily business as a page. When you don't show up in Sherwood, Robin Hood will come and rescue her. And you tell yourself he'll manage just fine without you. The castle is beginning to bustle with preparations for the wedding, so you're twice as busy as ever.

Then, one morning, very early, you are awakened by shouts and the clang of steel on steel. You stumble into your clothes and realize what is happening: Robin Hood and his men are attacking the castle!

You dash out into the hallway—and run smack into Little John!

"Oh, there you are!" he gasps. "It's a good thing I've found you—follow me!"

If you go with Little John, turn to page 78.

If you try to get away from him, turn to page 87.

King Richard must be warned. You put the soup down in front of Prince John. "Compliments of the chef," you say. "It's her specialty, mock turtle."

As you hurry down to the low table, you hear Prince John saying, "I've always wondered, Sheriff. What's *in* mock turtle soup?"

Pretending to refill Richard's wine cup, you whisper, "Your Majesty, the prince grows suspicious. Take care."

"I will," the king whispers. Then another friar calls you to serve him. When you look again, King Richard is gone.

Suddenly you see an old man beckoning to you from a doorway. Curious, you follow him out into the empty hallway. "Who are you?" you ask.

"I am called Nilrem," he tells you. "I have been following your adventures, and I am very pleased with you. You have done what you were brought here to do. Thanks to you, King Richard will escape his evil brother. And with the king's help, Robin will rescue Maid Marian."

"But I hardly did anything," you say modestly.

"That is for wiser heads than yours to judge," says Nilrem. "And now, farewell. Close your eyes and return to your own time."

The End

Little John leads you to the outlaw camp, where the attack on Nottingham Castle is being planned. You meet the rest of Robin Hood's band, who welcome you into their number.

Go on to the next page.

You recognize some of the famous ones: Alan-a-Dale, Friar Tuck, and Will Scarlett. The only one missing is Robin himself. But soon he arrives, leading a tall knight in black-plumed armor.

"What cheer!" Robin calls out. "I have a guest for dinner, a stranger I found wandering in Sherwood Forest. But since he will not remove his visor to show his face, he must needs eat through the helmet!"

"A stiff-necked soul," says Will Scarlett. "Perhaps he would like to try a game of buffets for the privilege of seeing his face."

Friar Tuck explains to you that in a game of buffets each man must stand still while the other one tries to knock him down with one blow.

"It would have to be a fair face indeed for me to risk being struck by such a big man," Alan-a-Dale says. But the others are eager to try their strength, and the Black Knight agrees to the trial.

One by one Robin and his men are defeated by the stranger. Even Little John, who seems so big, is sent staggering backward.

Finally, you're the only one left who hasn't tried.

If you challenge the Black Knight,
turn to page 60.

If you try to think of an excuse not to fight him,
turn to page 51.

His reflexes honed by years of battle, the Black Knight turns sharply to look for the danger. And while he is off-balance, you give him a push, sending him crashing to the ground.

The outlaws go wild—laughing, cheering, slapping you on the back. "A merry jest!" cries Friar Tuck. "God will forgive the deceit. As the Holy Word tells us, 'Wisdom cometh out of the mouths of babes.'"

"Does it, indeed?" asks the knight. "And doesn't it also say, 'Never strike thy king?'"

"Well, no," says Tuck. "That's just common sense. Who would—" He stops abruptly as the knight removes his helmet.

"Yes, indeed," the knight says, laughing. "It is I, King Richard Lionheart, returned from the Crusades to see that justice is done in fair England. Now, if someone will help me up, I'll begin by pardoning all of you, especially this clever child. And then I'd like to know why such gallant men live as outlaws in Sherwood Forest!"

Robin Hood tells the king all about the injustices that have been going on. King Richard is outraged, and says that if Robin will help him put things right, they will begin by rescuing Marian.

With brave King Richard on your side, you feel sure that all will go well now, and that the story will have a happy ending.

The End

You take Clarence by the shoulder. "Clarence," you tell him, "some things are more important than personal safety. Marian doesn't *want* to marry Sir Guy. She wants to live free in the greenwood with Robin Hood. And you and I are going to help her."

Clarence looks very pale. "I can't," he says. "You see—Sir Guy is my cousin. I'm Clarence of Gisborne."

You try to run, but the other pages tackle you.

"You were a good friend," Clarence says sadly. "I'm sorry you turned out to be a spy."

The sheriff locks you up in the deepest, darkest dungeon, with only spiders for company. Even if Robin attacks the castle, he may never find you here.

The End

"Sir," you say to Robin Hood. "Let me come with you. I'm the newest of the band, and I could watch for spies without being recognized."

Robin accepts your offer, and while you both change into beggars' rags, he explains that it is the custom for beggars to sit on the church steps and hold out a bowl for people to drop coins into. You don't understand how this is going to help distribute gold to the poor. But Robin smiles and tells you that you'll see soon enough.

After a long walk through the forest, you come to the town of Brampton. It isn't what *you* would call a town: just a dozen huts, a church, and a blacksmith's shop.

Robin sits down on the church steps and holds out his begging bowl. But it is full of coins! And instead of putting money into it as they pass by, the poor peasants take Robin's coins *out!* All the while Robin is calling out, "Alms for the poor! Help for a poor man down on his luck!" And you are watching to see if there's anything suspicious going on.

Out of the corner of your eye, you notice a well-dressed man lurking at the side of the church. It seems as though he's trying to watch Robin without being seen. Is he the spy Friar Tuck heard about? Maybe you'd better warn Robin, so he can escape.

Suddenly the man slips away toward the forest. Maybe it would be better for you to follow him. That way you'll know for certain what he's up to.

Go on to the next page.

If you decide to tell Robin Hood about the man, turn to page 46.

If you'd rather follow the man, turn to page 81.

Silently you wait in the tree for the tax collector's decision. "Oh, very well," he says at last. "The sooner we get through the woods, the sooner I'll sit down to a nice hot meal. But be on the lookout for outlaws!"

As the last guard passes under the shadow of your tree, you raise the whistle to your lips and blow a delicate birdcall.

You hear the answering signal repeated three times. Not long after you hear shouting. But soon it is quiet, and John gives the call for all-is-well.

Back at the camp, you find that Little John has returned the guards to Nottingham, tied backward on their horses. He has invited the tax collector to the noontime feast, since, as he puts it, " 'tis your own gold that pays for it!"

The terrified tax collector says he is not hungry.

"Suit yourself," says John. "There's many a poor soul that's hungry enough, because of the likes of you."

Little John ties the man to a tree, and the rest of you sit down to enjoy an excellent meal. Not bad for your first morning's work as an outlaw of Sherwood Forest!

The End

You set off down the road with your new companion. He tells you he's called Raven, and you can see why. His black hair shines like a raven's wing.

You make your way slowly toward Nottingham, stopping often to play for people in exchange for food or coins. True to his word, Raven gives you lessons on the harp. It's much harder than it looks! It has twenty-five strings, and your fingers keep getting lost and you play the wrong notes. But Raven is very patient. He also teaches you songs, by speaking the words and picking out the tunes on his harp. He says your voice is "not bad," and sometimes he lets you sing for money. But he never, ever sings himself.

One day you're having a very hard time learning a song. It's a wedding song, and Raven wants you to be able to perform it at Nottingham Castle. But you just can't get the tune right. Finally, in exasperation, he snaps at you, "No, no! It goes like this—listen—"

He opens his mouth to sing, but the sound that comes out is like a cross between a donkey braying and fingernails scratching on a blackboard.

It sounds, in fact, a lot like a raven's croak.

Raven glares at you as if he could read your thoughts. "And that," he says, "was not even a very good joke when *she* thought of it."

"*Who* thought of it?" you demand. "What are you talking about? What happened to your voice?"

Turn to page 86.

You stare at the woman hanging from the beam. She is as small and lithe as a boy. "Good grief!" you exclaim. "*You* can't be Maid Marian! Why, she's just some—"

"Some silly grown-up lady?" She does a double flip onto the floor.

Go on to the next page.

"Nevertheless, I am the Lady Marian. And I *was* silly enough to get caught spying. Now I'm stuck in this tiny room! I'll lose all the strength in my bow arm if I don't exercise. I just hope the loom doesn't break."

"Fear not!" you cry in your best heroic manner. "You will not be here much longer. I come from— mmph!" Marian has stuck her hand over your mouth.

"I can guess who you come from," she whispers, trying not to laugh, "and so will the guard outside, if you're not careful. Come over by the window and tell me all."

You explain everything. But when she hears the plan she says, "Isn't that just like Little John, rushing in without thinking things through! Robin would never have allowed it. How can I go free, leaving you here in danger? The sheriff is a cruel man. When he finds out you've tricked him, his wrath could be terrible!"

"I'm not afraid," you say, wishing your knees didn't feel quite so weak.

Marian is frowning in concentration. "There *must* be another way to do this."

If you agree that she can't just leave you there, turn to page 48.

If you insist that she escape now, turn to page 33.

You follow Little John down the hall. It is full of people fighting each other: outlaws in Lincoln green are hand to hand with the sheriff's guards. The hall is smoky, too. Part of the castle must be on fire! People are shrieking, and the floor is wet with water and blood.

In the confusion you lose Little John. You're trying to escape from the chaos when you feel a terrible pain in your chest. The last thing you see is the dagger in your heart. You'll never even know which side it was that killed you.

The End

Next to come along the road is an enormous train of knights, nobles, and servants, following a man wearing a crown. A herald is calling, "Make way for His Highness, Prince John!"

You give the signal, and Robin Hood, King Richard, and the other "friars" tag onto the end of the procession. Sure enough, you walk right into Nottingham Castle with Prince John and his followers.

At dinner, you sit in the great hall at the opposite end from Prince John and the sheriff of Nottingham. King Richard keeps his monk's hood over his head, but you notice Prince John looking at him strangely. Suddenly John calls to him, "Come here, Sir Friar!"

Richard goes to him. Prince John looks under his hood and cries, "Guards! Throw this man in the dungeon! His very looks speak treason!"

Before anyone can make a move, the true king is hustled off to the dungeons. With Richard gone and so many guards present, it is too risky to fight now. By stealth and cunning Robin manages to free Marian from the tower, but you all return to Sherwood Forest in a grim and worried state. It will take all your strength and careful planning to free Richard from the heavily guarded dungeon.

The End

Before the guard can stop you, you blow your birdcall whistle loudly, many times, so the outlaws will know you're in trouble.

"A signal!" the captain cries. "There must be more of them in Sherwood! Out with your swords, men!"

For a moment, all is still in the forest. You begin to think no one will come. Then an arrow whistles out from among the trees and lands right beside you. Wisely, the outlaws are staying in the woods. That way the horsemen can't get at them without being an easy target for their bows.

Realizing Little John's plan, the captain scoops you up and sets you in front of him on his horse. Now your friends can't shoot at him without risk of harming you.

"Let the youth go and we'll cease shooting!" Little John shouts from the woods.

"Never!" the captain calls back. "Your friend goes to Nottingham to be hanged as an example to all outlaws!"

Quickly Little John shoots an arrow low to spook the horse and keep the captain from riding away with you. It only grazes the horse's skin. But maddened by fear and pain, the animal plunges wildly—and John's next arrow accidentally takes you in the chest.

The screams you hear are your own.

The End

You follow the man you think is a spy—past the edge of town and all the way to an old, deserted mill. You creep up to a crack in the wall and listen as he tells someone, "The outlaw Robin Hood is in Brampton now, disguised as a beggar. Move swiftly and you will capture him—and I will have my reward!"

The old mill is very dusty. Before you can stop yourself, you give a triple sneeze.

Immediately strong hands seize you and haul you inside. "A spy!" the men exclaim. They tie you up and put a gag in your mouth. "The sheriff has no room in his jail for children," they sneer. "We'll release you once we have taken the outlaw Robin Hood."

But the man you followed leans over and whispers, "You will never be released. No one must know that it was I who betrayed Robin."

Night falls, and then another day comes. The mill is full of mice. By the time anyone looks for you here, all they will find is your bones.

The End

You bid the minstrel farewell and walk until you come to the ford. There stands a knight dressed head to toe in dark red armor. His sword is out, and he's blocking the way across the river.

"Good morning," you say politely. "How's it going?"

The knight's visor is closed so you can't see his face. Inside the helmet his voice booms hollowly. "Ho, there, coward! Do you yield?"

"Yield?!" you exclaim. "I didn't even know we were fighting! What is this, anyway? Why are you blocking the ford?"

"None shall pass by," the knight announces, "unless he beat me in single combat, or give in to my superior strength. In view of your small size, I offer you the chance to yield now, without bloodshed."

"Oh, you do, do you?" you mutter. This bully needs to be taught a lesson! "I choose to fight," you say. "Lend me a sword, and let's get going."

The knight gives you a big heavy sword, and you notice that although he is taller and stronger than you, in his armor he moves very slowly. As he lifts his arms to swing at you, you duck under his sword and push him right into the stream!

The red knight lies in the shallow water, splashing and waving his arms and legs like a turtle on its back, unable to get up without help.

"I hope you rust!" you say. And you cross the stream on your way to more adventures.

The End

The way north to Scotland is long and hard. But with courage and determination you lead the people of Brampton safely there, and in the wild hills you find a land to call your own.

The people have elected you as their leader. It is a great responsibility. As a person from the twentieth century, you are shocked by the cruelty and injustice of this time. You can't do much about the lack of medicine or machines, but you can learn from the mistakes of history yet to come. Under your leadership the people found New Brampton, a democratic cooperative where men and women have equal rights, everyone shares in the work, no one ever goes hungry, and children don't have to go to bed unless they're tired.

Have you changed the course of history by establishing the first democracy in England? Or will your achievement simply disappear in the mists of time?

The End

You and Robin Hood gratefully accept Brother Sebastian's offer of escape through the tunnel. He claims that no one else knows about it, so it should be safe from Robin's enemies. The monk will only take you one at a time, and Robin decides to go first—just in case there's anything funny going on. He follows the old man down the steps and out of sight.

After a while, Brother Sebastian comes back. "Your friend is safe," he says. "Now follow me."

The tunnel is pitch black. "I know my way in the dark after all these years," he explains. "But if you like, I will light a candle for you."

When you see where you are, you let out a shriek. You are surrounded by piles of skulls and bones! Empty eyes and lipless mouths grin at you everywhere. You take a step backward and tip over an entire pile. Bones come crashing down around you.

"What have you done to my brothers?" cries the old monk. "The bones of monks have rested in this charnel house for centuries. You have disturbed the peace of those who sleep here. Now you must pay for your crime!" He blows out the candle and scuttles away, leaving you in utter darkness.

"No, wait," you cry. But the mad old monk has abandoned you to a living tomb.

Turn to page 90.

Raven puts down his harp to tell you the story.

"The queen of the Fair Folk is a beautiful lady with good taste in music and a nasty temper. Once I was known as the greatest singer in the land. Then the queen herself came to me and by magic took me away to her court to sing for her. I served her seven years, and at the end of that time I begged to be allowed to return to the world of men. In a rage she let me go. But she vowed that I would never sing again as I had sung for her." Raven sighs. "Her magic is a powerful thing, as you yourself should know."

"Why me?" you ask.

"I may have lost my voice," he answers, "but I haven't lost my sight, nor yet my reason. I've been watching you for days. You're not stupid, but I've had to explain things to you that any three-year-old should know. It's perfectly plain that this is not your world and that the Fair Folk have brought you here." He clears his throat. "And now that you're here, I wish you would pay some attention to learning the wedding song, or we will both starve when we get to Nottingham!"

It's clear that Raven doesn't want to say any more about the Fair Folk—whoever they might be. But if he's right, and they really did bring you here by magic, then you need to know more so you can get back home.

Turn to page 110.

As soon as Little John gets far enough ahead, you drop back. He's running so fast he doesn't even notice. All around you people are screaming and slicing each other with swords and knives. Blood is everywhere. It's the worst thing you've ever seen. You feel sick to your stomach and scared to death.

In the last few days you've really gotten to know your way around the castle, and Clarence once showed you a secret underground passage that leads outside the castle walls. You use it now and escape into the forest. If only you could go home . . .

You wander through the woods, and soon you are completely lost. But at least no one is killing anybody here. You walk for hours, hungry and tired. Then you see it: a grassy clearing with a ring of flowers—the fairy ring! You go right to the middle of it and lie down, listening to the hum of bees growing louder and louder.

As you fall asleep, you think how happy your parents will be when you tell them you want to become a doctor. Of course, you'll never be able to explain how you first got the idea. . . .

The End

"Whoops!" you say, dropping the bowl of soup all over wicked Prince John. The soup is very thick—and very hot.

"Imbecile!" the sheriff of Nottingham yells at you. He mops at the prince with his enormous silk handkerchief. You try to "help" and succeed in getting more soup over everyone. The sheriff hits you with his wet hankie. "Clumsy oaf!"

"It was an accident," you protest.

"Accidents shouldn't happen to the king of England," snarls Prince John. "Yes, *King*—I said it and I mean it!" He rises and addresses the whole gathering.

Go on to the next page.

"By royal proclamation, I, John Plantagenet, declare myself king of England—and my brother Richard an outlaw! Furthermore, I set a price on his head: one thousand gold marks, dead or alive!"

In the shocked silence, the "friar" rises to speak. "A fair prize," he says. "Let me be the first to claim it, though a thousand marks suit this head not half as well as the crown of England, brother!" He throws back his robe to reveal a suit of armor.

"Richard!" shrieks the prince. "Capture him, men!"

The hall is suddenly bristling with the sheriff's guards. You're determined to fight alongside the king, but you have to admit the odds aren't exactly promising.

Turn to page 111.

You are alone in the tunnel. You can't see anything. You're afraid to move, afraid to reach out your hand, because you might touch a skull or a pile of bones. In the utter blackness, you can't even find your way back to the stairs leading to the church.

If you scream for help, no one will hear you through the stone. You do it anyway. There's no answer. Then you just scream. And scream. And scream.

Turn to page 118.

You take out your camera. If you stay in the shadow of the wall, maybe no one will notice you.

You look through the viewfinder. The procession is so large, you'll have to take several shots to get it all in. You click and click away—until you feel a hand on your shoulder.

"What toy is this, young page?" a guard asks.

"Umm . . . it's an Instamatic," you say nervously.

"Some Latin word, perhaps," he says. "I've no learning, not like you great folk. Well, get along to your duties. You'll have a chance to look at the prince at dinner."

You're so nervous, you can't keep from fiddling with the camera. Without meaning to, you push a button and the flash goes off! In the dark shadows, it seems very bright.

"Sorcery!" the guard shouts. "Help, ho! A plot to assassinate the prince!"

Your trial comes between the dancing bear and dinner. The sheriff is impatient to get back to his important guest and start eating, so he makes it short. "Because of your youth, I will be merciful," he says. "You will be hanged immediately instead of burned at the stake."

The End

You return to Sherwood Forest with Robin and the people of Brampton. Everything is fine for a while. Then, as winter draws on, there is hardship. The outlaws find it difficult to feed and shelter so many people. But the villagers are afraid to return to Brampton because the sheriff has promised to hang them all as conspirators.

There isn't much to do in the evening but sit around the fire, singing songs and telling stories to cheer yourselves up. In your day, with television for entertainment, you didn't need to be very good at storytelling. So you don't have much to contribute. But you get tired of being left out, so one night you tell a few elephant jokes. To your surprise, everyone nearly dies laughing! It turns out that all your old jokes are new to these people, and they think knock-knocks are the funniest thing going.

Suddenly you have a solution to the problem: you and the people of Brampton can become traveling entertainers! The sheriff will never find you, and you won't be dependent on Robin Hood and his men.

Your plan is a great success. Your traveling troupe becomes popular throughout England, and you become well known for your humor and wit. You're not worried about running out of funny stuff, either. After all, if they liked your elephant jokes, just wait till you introduce them to the custard-pie-in-the-face routine!

The End

The longer you can keep Sir Guy waiting outside your door, the more time Marian will have to get away from the castle. "Guy," you call. "I've got a surprise for you! But you'll have to be patient and wait an hour."

"Oh, my darling," he cries. "I've been waiting five long years for you. Another hour seems an eternity! But never mind. I will use the time to compose my hundredth poem to your beautiful eyes."

Oh, brother, you think. No wonder Marian doesn't want to marry him! You lower the rope out of the window. Sure enough, it isn't long enough. It's a good thing you didn't try to escape that way.

After an hour Sir Guy starts banging on the door again. Surely by now Marian is safely away. You tell the guards to let him in.

"Surprise!"

Turn to page 102.

"Sheriff," you say, "I'll tell you the truth. I'm not really a witch at all. I only said I was because I knew those guards were too stupid to understand the truth—not like you. Obviously you are intelligent and sophisticated, a man of the world."

Of course you lie. But the sheriff seems to like your flattery. "I'm really a powerful *scientist*," you continue. "It's not the same thing at all—as you know."

"No, of course not," says the sheriff, not wishing to appear a fool. "But can a scientist help me to get power beyond my wildest dreams?"

"Well . . . yes and no. I can give you the power of *knowledge*," you say, embarrassed to find yourself talking just like one of your teachers. "And that's more than anyone else around here seems to have."

"Give me an example," he demands.

You show the sheriff how the flash on your camera works. When he asks for an explanation you use every big word you know. He is impressed and gives you your own tower room for scientific research. Everything will be fine until the batteries of your camera run out. Then maybe you can explain to him about static electricity. With 800 years of scientific knowledge behind you, all you have to do now is remember everything you learned in school.

The End

You concentrate on the image of the hallway. You see it so clearly you might almost be there. You feel something hard under your feet . . . stone . . . you *are* there! You hear footsteps and shrink against the wall. But it's only someone about your age, dressed in a kind of uniform. The kid looks really familiar. But you don't know anybody in this world, and it isn't someone from camp.

The kid stares at you and says, "Who are you?"

Go on to the next page.

You decide to play it safe. "I'm Raven the minstrel's apprentice," you reply. "Who're you?"

"I'm just a page," the other kid answers quickly. "Nobody important. Actually, I'm, um, supposed to take something to Maid Marian, who's locked up in the tower. Do you know where she is?"

"No," you say. "Sorry, I don't."

The page looks at you hard. "Don't I know you from somewhere?"

"I don't think so," you reply.

The page hurries off down the hall. Suddenly you realize why the face was familiar: It's *yours!* Maybe if you'd hunted the arrow by day you'd have ended up as a page in a castle helping Robin Hood get Maid Marian out of a tower. Maybe this is the answer to the riddle.

You close your eyes—and when you open them you're standing in front of the queen of the Fair Folk. You tell her the answer to the riddle and she smiles. "Well done! And now, farewell, mortal child! For I always keep my bargains."

You hear a rushing sound like the wind, mixed with silver bells. Everything is blurry. When you can see again you realize that you're in your own living room at home.

"Hello, dear," your parents say. "How was camp?"

The End

While Robin Hood escapes into the church, you run to the blacksmith's shop and grab an iron bar. Waving it, you yell at the top of your lungs, "People of Brampton! Will you let the sheriff's men arrest your friend? How long must this tyranny continue? Attack them, I say, and long live Robin Hood!"

"Long live Robin Hood!" the people cry. "Down with the sheriff and his men!" They grab bars, poles, rakes—even brooms—and attack the horsemen. You lead them, shouting all the best slogans you remember from history: "Give me liberty or give me death! Don't fire till you see the whites of their eyes! Liberty, equality, fraternity!" It doesn't seem to matter that they are centuries ahead of their time. The people rally to your cause and chase the sheriff's men out of town.

Robin Hood comes out of the church. "For one who came in peace for all mankind, you are a mighty warrior!" he tells you. Then he warns the people of Brampton that the sheriff will soon send more soldiers to punish them for their rebellion. They must go into hiding.

The people want you as their leader. Some of them want to go north into the hills of Scotland and found a new village there. Others want to hide in Sherwood Forest until the sheriff has forgotten his wrath.

If you choose to lead the villagers into Scotland, turn to page 83.

If you prefer to return to Sherwood Forest, turn to page 92.

You can see the old man across the fire perfectly clearly. He's still smiling at you, so you go over to talk to him.

"Greetings, my child," he says. "I see you have found the way here. You must be brave, now, and strong and cunning. Do not forget your oath to Robin Hood. But if your courage should fail you, call upon the Words of Power to return you to your native land."

"What words of power?" you say. "I don't know any magic."

"They are words of your own making, bitter words of unhappiness. Use them only as a last resort."

You still don't know what he means. But before you can ask, a spark jumps out of the fire and lands in the dry grass near your feet. You hurry to step on it, and when you look up, the old man is gone.

Turn to page 22.

"Stand back," you call to Marian. "I'm going to break the door down!" You pick up a pikestaff one of the guards left behind. But before you can attack the door with it, Robin Hood comes running up the stairs.

"Stand back," he calls to Marian. "I'm going to break the door down!"

All right, you shrug; *he's* the hero around here.

With one blow of his shoulder the door shivers. With a second blow it cracks on its hinges. Marian squeezes out through the crack. When she hears what's happening, she insists on going downstairs to join the fighting.

You go down to find that the battle is already over, and the victory is Richard's. Everyone cheers when they see you with Robin and Marian.

King Richard pardons all the outlaws and sends Prince John and his followers to the dungeons in chains. To you the king says, "I owe you my life. If you accept a position in my court, you shall serve at my side and learn all noble skills: hunting, dancing, falconry, music . . . even reading and writing, if you desire it!"

"Well . . ." You hesitate, thinking of home.

"Your clothes shall be of the finest satin and velvet," continues the king. "Many servants will wait upon you. And I shall give you a swift horse from my stable and a fine hound from my kennels."

You accept.

The End

At first Sir Guy is furious. But after a while he calms down, and you are able to explain that Marian really isn't his type.

"Well, I *did* find her a little, ah, energetic and, er, hot-tempered," he admits. "But I was sure she'd settle down once we were married."

"Never," you say firmly. "You would have made each other miserable."

"That may be so," he says sadly, "but I will love her forever. And if I can't have her, I shall marry no other."

Your mission is accomplished: You've freed Marian. But now you feel sorry for Guy! So you offer to keep him company for a while. As it turns out, when he's not being mushy about his lost love, he's a pretty nice guy, and the two of you become good friends. He never does marry, and when he dies he makes you his heir.

The End

Your nose is full of water, you're sinking . . . sinking. Then you hear a voice shouting, "Kick! Kick!"

You kick and realize that there are no longer any skirts entangling your legs. You come to the surface, gasping for air—and see the Camp Yoo-chee-Koowee swim coach.

"Stroke! Kick!" he yells at you. "Honestly, how are you ever going to learn if you don't follow instructions?"

It's the first time you've ever been glad to see the swim coach.

The End

Little John gets a set of old-woman's clothes from a farm wife. They are sizes too large, so you pad them with rags and with a nice long rope for tying up guards or climbing down towers. You put on a bonnet, darken your face with berry juice, and draw on age lines with charcoal.

Little John takes you as far as the walls of Nottingham Castle. Then he gives your shoulder a squeeze of encouragement and melts into the crowd. You totter up to the gate.

"What can I do for you, grandmother?" asks a guard.

Your disguise is working! You smother a smile and start to wail and carry on. "Oh, my lady. My little Marian, who I nursed since she was a baby. To see her in such a dreadful place! It breaks my poor heart."

The guard isn't a bad sort. "There, now," he says. "Don't take on so. I tell you what: I'll take you to visit her."

"Oh, thank you," you snivel. "Ever since she joined that awful outlaw Robin Hood I haven't heard a word from her—not even a postcard. Maybe now she'll see the error of her ways."

You follow the guard into the castle and up a winding stair to the tower. Suddenly he freezes. A fat man is coming toward you, and he looks meaner than the swim coach at Camp Yoochee-Koowee. "Curtsey!" hisses the guard.

You try a trembling curtsey—and fall flat on your face. The fat man laughs hysterically. When he finally can speak, he demands, "Who are you?"

If you pretend you're a clown and fell on purpose, turn to page 24.

If you act like Marian's old nurse, turn to page 27.

106

You dash back down the stairs, determined to make the sheriff give you the keys to Marian's cell. You're running so fast your feet slip out from under you. CRACK! Your head strikes the stone steps, and darkness claims you forever.

The End

Somehow you manage to limp back to camp and find your way to the infirmary. Of course no one believes your story. They think you're delirious with fever or shock. The security guards look for the intruder anyway—but they never find him. Soon even you begin to wonder if you didn't just imagine the whole thing. But you couldn't have shot yourself, could you?

The kids are nicer to you now that you're in the infirmary. A girl named Lucy brings you a pile of books to read. You pick one up—and stare in shock at the cover. It's a picture of the man in the forest! The book is *The Adventures of Robin Hood.*

Maybe when you get better you'll try going out on another moonlit night, just to see what happens. And maybe you'll even take Lucy with you.

The End

Up is probably the direction you need to go to find Maid Marian's tower cell. But the stairs only lead to another corridor. Suddenly you see someone standing in the hall. You blink. No one was there a moment ago!

"Who are you?" you ask.

"Raven the minstrel's apprentice," is the reply.

The stranger is just a kid and seems to be as lost as you are. But just in case, you say, "I'm, um, supposed to take something to Maid Marian. Do you know where she is?"

"No, sorry, I don't." The young minstrel stares at you. "Don't I know you from somewhere?"

Go on to the next page.

The apprentice is about your age and does look oddly familiar. But you can't possibly know anyone here, and you don't have any time to waste. "I don't think so," you say, and you hurry off down the hall looking for the stairs to the tower.

You can still taste the rose water in your mouth. You wish you could brush your teeth. But you've never heard of a medieval toothbrush—let alone toothpaste.

Suddenly you realize where you've seen that kid before: in the bathroom mirror, brushing *your* teeth! The minstrel looks just like you! Either you've got a twin here, or somehow you've met yourself having a different adventure. You rush back to the hallway, but the apprentice is gone.

You continue to search, but there's no sign of Maid Marian or your "twin." So at last you go back down the stairs and open the door you passed up in favor of the staircase.

Turn to page 41.

"If these so-called Fair Folk brought me here from the future, I'll just have to get them to send me back," you say firmly.

"Don't even *think* about trying to make them do anything," says Raven. "They are powerful and full of strange jests. I tried to make them return me to earth, and look what they did to me!"

"Yes," you say, "and it was a rotten thing to do. We've got to find some way to make them give you back your voice."

Raven smiles sadly. "Child, you have already been touched by fairy magic. Do not—"

"*Fairies?*" you cry. "Is that what the 'Fair Folk' are—just a bunch of fairies? Little things with wings that sit around on mushrooms and talk to butterflies? That stuff's for kids."

Suddenly you hear a sweet jingling sound. Coming toward you across the field is a beautiful woman on a white horse. The horse's bridle is strung with hundreds of tiny silver bells. "Mortal child," she says in a scornful voice, "what is your business with the Fair Folk's queen?"

She doesn't have wings, and she wouldn't fit on a mushroom, and her expression is anything but sweet. But she does seem to have come in answer to your wishes.

If you decide to ask her to take the spell off Raven's voice, turn to page 15.

If you decide to ask her how to get back to your own time, turn to page 116.

Just when you think all is lost, the other friars throw off their robes. They're dressed in Lincoln green—it's Robin Hood and his men! "Down with Prince John!" they shout, rallying around the king.

"Robin Hood!" cries the sheriff of Nottingham. "Five hundred marks to the man who brings me his carcass!"

The hall turns into a battlefield. John's men outnumber the outlaws, but many people hate the prince and are going over to Richard's side.

With all the guards involved in the battle, now might be a good time to rescue Maid Marian. The sheriff is hiding under the table, and you threaten him with a turkey leg until he tells you where to find her.

Following the sheriff's directions, you race upstairs to Marian's tower cell. She's pounding on the door and yelling, "What's going on out there? Let me out!"

"Hang on," you call. "I've come to rescue you."

"Then hurry up and let me out," she replies.

Suddenly you realize you've forgotten the keys. You'll have to go back and get them from the sheriff. But maybe you can figure out how to break the door down instead.

If you go back for the keys, turn to page 106.

If you try to break down the door, turn to page 101.

You take Robin Hood aside and say to him, "Let's stay where we are. I have a funny feeling about this friar guy. He seems kind of crazy to me."

"Yet I think we may trust him to carry a message to Sherwood, alerting my men to our plight," says Robin.

So that is what you do. Brother Sebastian disappears down the dark tunnel, but you leave the stone off the entrance to let in more fresh air.

The wait seems intolerable. You're feeling desperate enough to risk entering the tunnel, when the door crashes open and the soldiers come in. You and Robin fight valiantly, but the odds are against you. Just when all seems lost, you hear a hunting horn.

"It's my men!" Robin gasps. "Brother Sebastian has not failed us. Be strong—help is coming!"

Friar Tuck and a half dozen other outlaws come running to your aid. Together you defeat the soldiers. Then for good measure you steal their horses to ride back to Sherwood.

Robin tells everyone how brave you were. The outlaws are proud to have you among them, and you know that if this day is any indication, your stay in Sherwood Forest will be very exciting.

The End

"My powers are so great," you say, "I can call upon the sun at midnight."

"That is great, indeed," says the sheriff. But he sounds as if he doesn't believe you. "I will return at that hour to witness this great magic."

At midnight he and his guards come to your cell. "Show me the power of the sun," he demands.

You take out your camera, switch it to flash, and take his picture. When the flash goes off, the sheriff cringes from the glare. His guards duck, screaming, "Help! Witchcraft!"

But the evil sheriff recovers quickly. "Very good," he says. "But not quite good enough. You can call upon light at midnight, but you could not escape from this simple dungeon. Guards! Burn this imp."

You are dragged out to the courtyard and tied to a stake piled round with wood. Is there nothing that can save you? Even arts and crafts would be better than this!

Suddenly you remember the mysterious old man at Robin Hood's fire, the one Will Scarlett called Nilrem. Could he possibly help you?

If you spoke to him that night, turn to page 52.

If you ignored him, turn to page 30.

The "friars" fall in at the end of the caravan, while you stay up front—riding double with a chatty widow from Bath. She explains that along the way to Canterbury, the pilgrims are having a contest to see which one of them can tell the best story. Some of the tales are funny, some are sad. Some tell of warfare and adventure, some of love.

The story you're listening to is so exciting that you forget to pay attention to where you're going. When it ends, you look around and discover that the "friars" have all gone. The widow says you passed through Nottingham two hours ago!

You could walk back. But it would take forever on foot, and by the time you got there, the battle might be over. You decide to continue traveling with the pilgrims. If all the stories are as good as the last one, it will be fun. You can learn all about the people and their time—maybe even write down their stories and get extra credit in history, or English.

Of course, you'll have to tell a story yourself. Maybe you'll tell the magical tale of a person who is transported to Old England from the future . . . but will anyone believe it?

The End

Face to face with the queen of the Fair Folk, you're suddenly very polite. "Please, Your Majesty," you say, "if you brought me here from the twentieth century, how am I going to get back home?"

"I'll tell you if you can answer me a riddle," the beautiful lady replies.

You hear Raven mutter, "Oh, no, not that!" and you know this is going to be hard.

"Here is the riddle," says the queen: "You hunted under the rays of the moon. Where would you be now, if you had hunted under the rays of the sun?"

"That's not a riddle!" you cry. "It's not even funny!"

"Hush!" Raven hisses. "Don't anger her further. All the Fair Folk can see across time and know the answers to riddles like that. I *told* you not to meddle."

You try to think. What you hunted under the moonlight was your lost arrow. But how are *you* supposed to know what would have happened if you'd kept looking for it during the day?

"Think deeply," says the queen.

Your whole body starts to tingle, and strange images flash through your head. You see a stone hallway, and then you see the number three. Is this magic surrounding you?

Go on to the next page.

ABOUT THE AUTHOR

In between growing up in Cleveland, Ohio, and moving to New York City to be a writer, ELLEN KUSHNER attended Bryn Mawr College, where she appeared as Alan-a-Dale in the annual Robin Hood play. Her archery experience includes shooting holes in the side of a garage and into a plastic garbage can. She has worked as an editor for several New York publishers and now enjoys playing the guitar, feeding the cats, and getting letters from her readers.

ABOUT THE ILLUSTRATOR

JUDITH MITCHELL was born and raised in New York City. She earned a Bachelor of Fine Arts degree from Chatham College and has also studied art at the Columbia University School of Arts and at the School of Visual Arts, in New York City. Prints of her work are in considerable demand at science fiction and fantasy conventions around the country.

She enjoys music, animals, cooking, collecting antiques, and travel. She and her husband, Jack Murray, live in New York City with their three middle-aged cats.